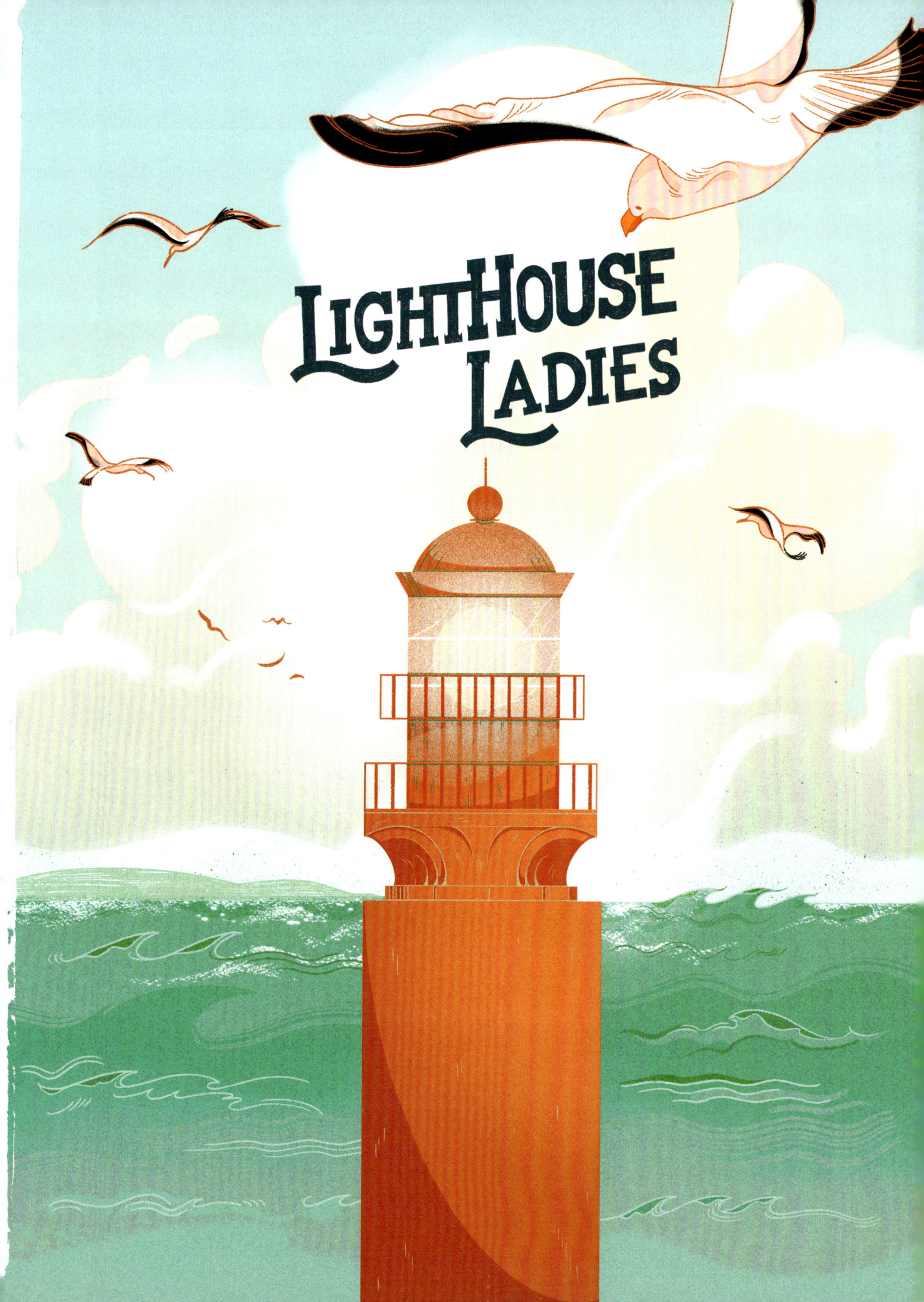

For Sean, Juniper, and Cora.
My guiding lights.
—K.C.

To my mother, Idelia.
Another woman whose
hard work shouldn't be
lost to history.
—I.M.

Clarion Books is an imprint of HarperCollins Publishers.
Lighthouse Ladies: Shining a Spotlight on Hardy
Heroines. Text copyright © 2025 by Kristin Quinn.
Illustrations copyright © 2025 by Islenia Mil. All rights
reserved. Manufactured in Capriate San Gervasio,
Italy. No part of this book may be used or reproduced
in any manner whatsoever without written
permission except in the case of brief quotations
embodied in critical articles and reviews. For
information address HarperCollins Children's Books,
a division of HarperCollins Publishers, 195 Broadway,
New York, NY 10007. www.harpercollinschildrens.com.
Library of Congress Control Number: 2024949639
ISBN 978-0-06-335183-7. The artist used Procreate
and Photoshop to create the digital illustrations
for this book. Typography by Celeste Knudsen.
25 26 27 28 29 RTLO 10 9 8 7 6 5 4 3 2 1
First Edition

Lighthouse Ladies

Shining a Spotlight on Hardy Heroines

Words by KRIS CORONADO

Art by ISLENIA MIL

CLARION BOOKS
An Imprint of HarperCollinsPublishers

TO MAN A LIGHTHOUSE over a century ago required **perseverance.**
Fortitude.
Courage.
A feat tackled by hundreds of salty souls across America.

Strapping and strong, these souls minded the blazing beacons that guided ships safely to shore. They were full of grit. Bravery personified.

By the way...

many weren't guys.

In a time when women were expected to stay at home to balance chores with children, these ladies defied convention with conviction. Their gazes swept across waters from Maine to Florida to California.

It was a life where stairs spiraled like a conch shell. Quarters were sometimes snug, and work wasn't a breeze. (Especially considering that many wore long skirts instead of pants!)

Nevertheless, the ocean called.

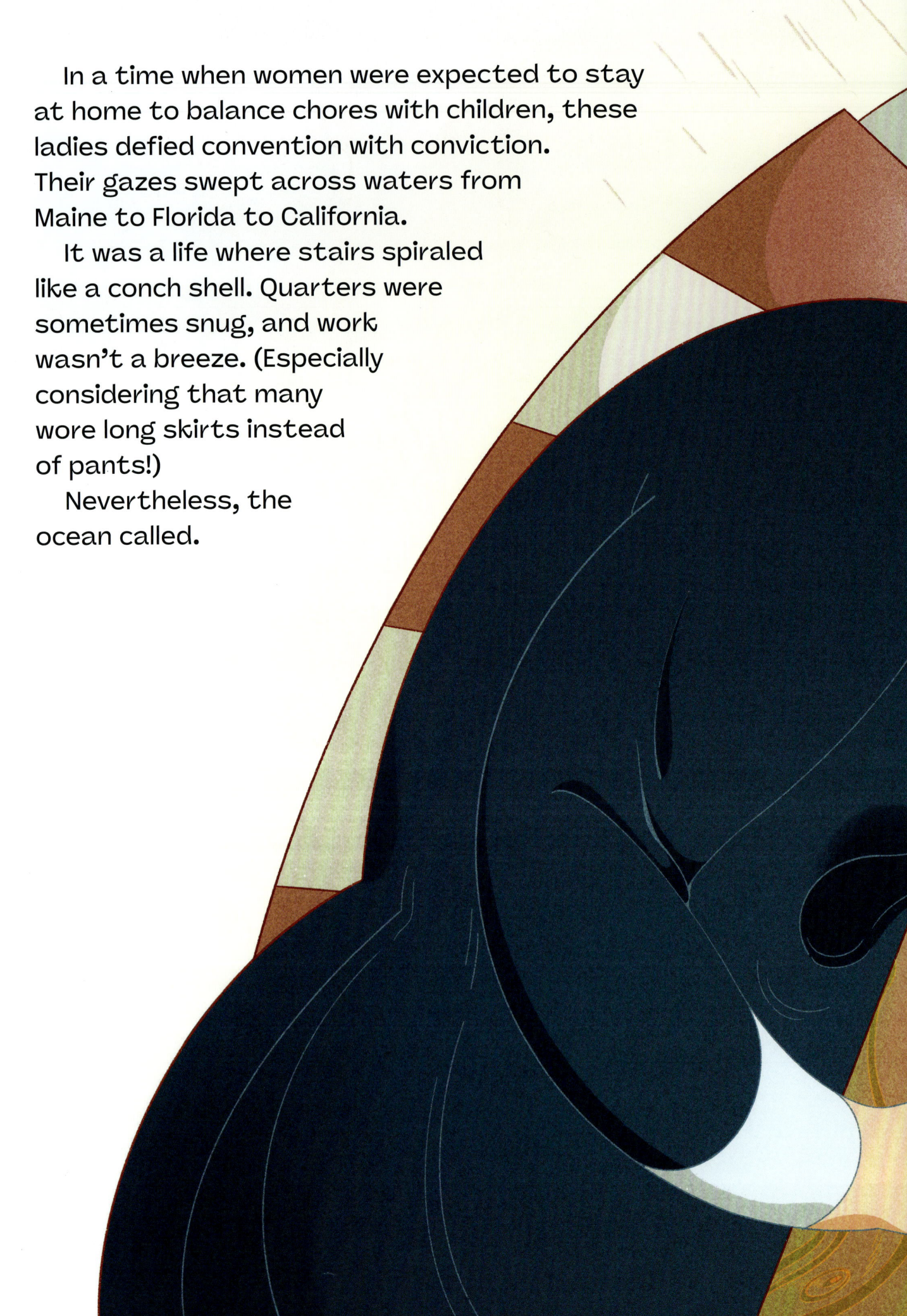

At sunrise, they extinguished lamps and polished them to a glittery sheen. They trimmed wicks to guarantee a steady and constant beam.

Logs were neatly kept. Floors were carefully swept.

ON THE EVENING OF MARCH 29, 1869, Ida Lewis felt sluggish and tired. Her head pounded like crashing waves. She needed rest. But the churning water had other plans. . . .

For even a bad cold couldn't anchor Ida when her mother saw something alarming in Rhode Island's Newport Harbor: "Ida, run quick, a boat capsized and men drowning, run quick, Ida!" No time for a hat! Or shoes! Ida called to her younger brother Hosea and told him what to do.

Brittle rocks sliced Ida's stockinged feet as she and Hosea plunged their rowboat into the frothy water.

Row!

Frigid saltwater smacked and whacked. Buckets of rain blocked their view.

Row!

With a precise stroke, Ida rotated the boat before they dragged the men inside.

Row!

The sea had met its match. Ida arm wrestled it with every pull.

Row!

Back to the Lime Rock Lighthouse
through biting cold. Two lives spared.
The episode, retold in newspapers
and magazines, made Ida famous.

It wasn't her first rescue, and it wasn't her last. In all her years of safeguarding, Ida saved at least eighteen people. (Although unofficial counts put the number at twenty-five!)

Of course, one didn't need to row a boat to save lives. . . .

MEET JULIET NICHOLS.
On July 2, 1906, woolly fog blanketed San Francisco Bay with thick, murky mist.
On a day when the broken fog bell at Point Knox Lighthouse was dangerously quiet, Juliet was not.

Wham! Wham!
Realizing that blinded ships
could smash against Angel
Island's jagged banks without a
warning, she grabbed a hammer.

Wham! Wham!
Juliet pounded her station's
gigantic bell with all her might
every fifteen seconds.

Wham! Wham!
Her arms aching, muscles
quaking . . .
Until the fog faded over
twenty hours later.
And the ships? Not a single
one wrecked!

Although, this wasn't Juliet's final battle with her foggy foe. Another time, she wound the fog bell every fifty minutes for three days! Even so, she couldn't imagine acting any other way: "It was nothing but my duty."

Duty indeed! Ladies like Juliet may not have needed to boast, but they rose to the occasion when it mattered the most. Even when navigating the impossible...

ON SUNSHINE-DAPPLED DAYS, ferry riders could count on a wave from "Aunt" Venus Parker as they headed to shore.

This was not one of those times.

Venus gazed at the frosty water around Killock Shoal Light. It was January 1912. She and her keeper husband, William, were stranded. Plunging temperatures had kept them cut off from land for weeks.

Supplies were dwindling. There was no time to lose.

Venus struck out alone in a small boat bound for Chincoteague, Virginia.

Crack! Icy channel water tried to stop her, but Venus was determined. She sliced through the unfriendly frigid air. She *had* to get there!

Reaching land safe and sound, Venus gathered what she needed.

Relief, however, was brief.
At sunset, Venus gazed across
the channel. The lighthouse was still
visible in the gathering darkness . . .
but why was there no light?
Something was not right.

Quick! With help from local men, Venus battled her way back across the water.

Her hands clenched the ladder reaching toward home.

Climb!

Climb!

Climb!

But oh!
  William had died while she
was gone. Despite her grief,
Venus needed to carry on.
  As his body was brought
back to shore, Venus stayed.
  Others needed her more.

Venus kept the light until a replacement keeper arrived. A courageous commitment day after day.

For others, living near a lighthouse's shadow was life's only way. . . .

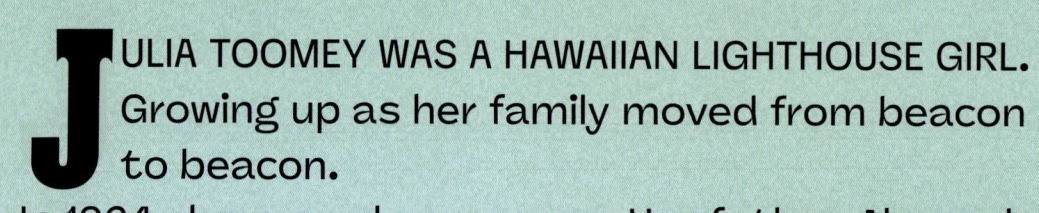

JULIA TOOMEY WAS A HAWAIIAN LIGHTHOUSE GIRL. Growing up as her family moved from beacon to beacon.

In 1924 she moved once more. Her father, Alexander, was appointed assistant keeper at Makapu'u Point.

Home was now tucked
atop a lava rock cliff.
Wind howled and waves
walloped below.

A secluded spot, yes.
A lonely one? No!

Heights were not feared, but
something familiar and dear.
Days frothed to the brim.
Racing
    up,
        up,
            up!
Racing
      down,
    down,
  down!

Helping Father keep the lens shipshape
so a gleaming beam could be seen for miles.

Rub,
  rub,
    rub!
One prism polished to rainbow-glow
perfection... over a thousand more to go!

On weekends, loads of visiting friends. Fun seemingly without an end.

Splash!

Frolic!

Fish!

Hurry, send Sport to fetch Father for the haul!

A beachy dream had by all. Golden days framed by dazzling blue. Legs tickled by yellow ilima too.

Until . . .

The ultimate sacrifice.
Father saved the light . . .
but paid with his life.

His parting words: "Stand by the
light and keep it burning."
Mother heartbroken. Father gone.

The light kept burning.
But sometimes being a hardy
lighthouse lady meant bravely moving on.

For bravery in a lighthouse lady was nothing new. Conquering challenges? Something to become accustomed to.

Onward each went. Mothers. Daughters. Wives. Tackling all kinds of obstacles, under all kinds of skies.

Some days were boring. Others were downright serene. (Well . . . for the most part.)

But these women thrived in their daily routines.

What some may call cramped could be quite cozy. What looked like challenging chores could be another's true calling.

There were big moments that shone brightly.

There were small pleasures that would endure too.

And quite often . . .

...there was an undeniable view.

AUTHOR'S NOTE

Fact: This book could have been ten times as long! While this true tale highlights four real women, many played important roles in keeping lighthouses shining bright over the centuries. Hannah Thomas was the first recorded American female lighthouse keeper. In 1776 she took charge of two towers located on Gurnet Point, in the colony of Massachusetts, when her husband left to fight in the American Revolution. You'll find her name and 174 other women listed on this United States Coast Guard Historian's Office website page: http://bit.ly/3YT8NZi. That's not even counting the wives and daughters who contributed immensely to what was often a family all-hands-on-deck way of life. "Those people weren't really paid, those wives and daughters, the family," says amateur lighthouse historian and author Elinor DeWire, who estimates there were over a thousand women who helped keep lighthouses. "They were expected to help." And help they did . . . and then some! In fact, Ida Lewis was not officially appointed keeper until 1879—ten years after the famous rescue described in this book! When her lightkeeper father became ill in 1857, Ida and her mother kept the light, although Ida did a big chunk of the work.

Ida Lewis on the cover of *Harper's Weekly* in 1869

In the coming years, more intriguing lighthouse ladies' stories will continue to be unearthed by writers, historians, and lighthouse enthusiasts. Astounding accounts like that of Kate Moore of Connecticut's Black Rock Harbor Lighthouse. After her father was appointed keeper in 1817, she began assisting him at age twelve and eventually took over his duties when his health declined. She saved twenty-three lives. For another Kate it was double that amount . . . and more! Kate Walker estimated that she'd "saved about fifty persons" while tending the light at Robbins Reef Lighthouse (between Staten Island and the Statue of Liberty) from 1886 to 1919. To learn more about these impressive women, check out this great catalog by the United States Lighthouse Society, which includes photos when available, here: https://archives.uslhs.org/taxonomy/term/497.

Today, the age of lighthouse keeping is over. As technology advanced and lighthouse operations became automated, the role of keepers was no longer necessary. Nevertheless, the last United States Coast Guard lighthouse keeper was a woman. Sally Snowman kept Boston Light from 2003 to 2023, after a law was passed in 1989 requiring the eighteenth-century lighthouse to maintain an attendant. "It is amazing to witness the calm before the storms and the storms, followed by awesome rainbows," Snowman said of her job in 2021. "With nature around me all the time, it clears the head and heals the soul."

Juliet Nichols depicted in the San Francisco Chronicle in 1906

ACKNOWLEDGMENTS

To the historians, writers, and enthusiasts who make up the lighthouse community I offer heartfelt thanks. Your feedback and guidance gave this book a firm foundation to build upon.

WHAT HAPPENED TO JULIA TOOMEY?

Julia Toomey's cousins standing before Makapu'u Point Lighthouse circa 1929. Courtesy of Ian Y. Lind

After Julia's dad, Alexander Toomey, died from burns resulting from an explosion at Makapu'u Point Lighthouse in April 1925, Julia's days of living near lighthouses came to an end. Sadly, her mother, Minnie, died only two months later—a day after giving birth to Julia's youngest sister, also named Minnie. Julia and her brother and sisters lived with relatives and friends in Honolulu.

Julia didn't talk about her lighthouse days much, says her daughter, Loke Kapela, who lives in Kailua-Kona, Hawaii. Even so, living along a lighthouse cliff had lasting effects: Julia had no fear of heights. "My mother, into her late sixties, climbed up a plumeria tree to get on the roof of our house to climb a bigger tree that was on the side of the house," says Loke. The larger tree was a mango tree, filled with delicious fruit her mom would pick.

As an adult, Julia worked as a telephone operator. She loved singing and dancing the Charleston and became a talented Hawaiian quilter. Of all the lighthouses she lived near, Diamond Head Lighthouse kept a special spot in her heart—the beach there was her favorite place in the world.

Makapu'u Point Lighthouse in March 2020. Courtesy of Jeffrey J. Davis (www.jeffreyjdavis.com)

QUOTE SOURCES

- "Ida, run quick, a boat capsized and men drowning, run quick, Ida!" —Brewerton, George D. *Ida Lewis: The Heroine of Lime Rock*, Newport, RI: A.J. Ward, 1869, 25.
- "It was nothing but my duty." —"The Real Heroine of Angel Island," *San Francisco Chronicle*, May 13, 1906, 12.
- "Stand by the light and keep it burning." —"Alexander D. Toomey," *Lighthouse Service Bulletin*, May 1925.
- "Those people weren't really paid, those wives and daughters, the family. They were expected to help." —Elinor DeWire, interview with author, July 7, 2023.
- "saved about fifty persons" —"Mrs. Walker Dies; Lighthouse Keeper," *New York Times*, Feb. 7, 1931, 12.
- "It is amazing to witness the calm before the storms and the storms, followed by awesome rainbows. With nature around me all the time, it clears the head and heals the soul." —Stoller, Gary, "How A Historic Lighthouse Changed the Life of Former College Professor," *Forbes*, Jan. 22, 2021.
- "My mother, into her late sixties, climbed up a plumeria tree to get on the roof of our house to climb a bigger tree that was on the side of the house." —Loke Kapela, interview with author, Aug. 24, 2022.

KILLOCK SHOAL LIGHT HOUSE, CHINCOTEAGUE, ACCOMAC CO. VA.

A postcard of Killock Shoal Light circa 1913. Courtesy of Kirk Mariner Collection, Eastern Shore of Virginia Heritage Center, Parksley, VA

SELECTED BIBLIOGRAPHY

"Alexander D. Toomey." *Lighthouse Service Bulletin*, May 1925.

"Black Rock Tower: The Ancient Dame Who Trimmed the Lights." *Ferndale Enterprise* (Ferndale, CA), Oct. 11, 1895, 3.

Carroll, Rick. "Makapuu Lighthouse Flashback – Glowing Joy and Fade – Out." *Honolulu Advertiser*, Aug. 10, 1985, 1.

"Certain Unsung Heroines." *Sioux City Journal* (Sioux City, IA), Mar. 5, 1916, 23.

"Chincoteague Light Keeper Found Dead at His Post." *Democratic Messenger* (Snow Hill, MD), Feb. 3, 1912, 5.

Chartier, JoAnn. "Juliet Fish Nichols: The Angel of Angel Island." *Lighthouse Digest*, Mar. 2005. Accessed Aug. 19, 2021. http://www.lighthousedigest.net/Digest/StoryPage.cfm?StoryKey=2185.

Clifford, J. Candace and Mary Louise. *Women Who Kept the Lights: An Illustrated History of Female Lighthouse Keepers*. Alexandria, VA: Cypress Communications, 2000.

Dean, Love. *The Lighthouses of Hawai'i*. Honolulu: University of Hawaii Press, 1991.

DeWire, Elinor. *Guardians of the Lights: Stories of U.S. Lighthouse Keepers*. Sarasota: Pineapple Press, 1995.

"Explosion at Makapu Point Lighthouse, Hawaii." *Lighthouse Service Bulletin*, June 1925.

"Heroism in the Lighthouse Service. A Description of Life on Matinicus Rock." *Century Illustrated Monthly Magazine*, London: Macmillan & Co. Ld., Vol. 54, May 1897, 219-225.

"Ida Lewis. The Grace Darling of America." *New York Tribune*, April 12, 1869, 7.

"Ida Lewis, the Newport Heroine." *Harper's Weekly*, July 31, 1869.

"Idawalley Zorada Lewis(-Wilson), Keeper, USLHS." United States Coast Guard Historian's Office. Accessed Sept. 2, 2021. https://www.history.uscg.mil/Browse-by-Topic/Notable-People/All/Article/186507/idawalley-zorada-lewis-wilson-keeper-uslhs.

"Lighthouse Keepers." National Park Service. Accessed Oct. 4, 2021. https://www.nps.gov/articles/lighthouse-keepers.htm.

Riddell, Shona. *Guiding Lights*. Dunedin, New Zealand: Exisle Publishing, 2020.

Skomal, Lenore. *The Lighthouse Keeper's Daughter: The Remarkable True Story of American Heroine Ida Lewis*. Guilford, CT: Globe Pequot Press, 2010.

Taylor, Stephen J. "Harriet Colfax, Guardian of the Indiana Shore." *Hoosier State Chronicles*, June 1, 2015. Accessed Sept. 14, 2021. https://blog.newspapers.library.in.gov/harriet-a-colfax.

"The Modern Grace Darling." *Harper's Weekly*, April 17, 1869.

"The Real Heroine of Angel Island." *San Francisco Chronicle*, May 13, 1906, 12.

United States Light-House Establishment. *Instructions and Directions to Light Keepers*. Sixth edition. Washington: Government Printing Office, Sept. 1871.

"Women Lighthouse Keepers: Breaking the Barrier: Women Lighthouse Keepers and Other Female Employees of the U.S. Lighthouse Board/Service." United States Coast Guard Historian's Office. Accessed Aug. 11, 2021. https://www.history.uscg.mil/Browse-by-Topic/Notable-People/Women/Women-Lighthouse-Keepers.